Dear Parents:

Congratulations! Your child is taking the first steps on an exciting journey. The destination? Independent reading!

STEP INTO READING® will help your child get there. The program offers five steps to reading success. Each step includes fun stories and colorful art or photographs. In addition to original fiction and books with favorite characters, there are Step into Reading Non-Fiction Readers, Phonics Readers and Boxed Sets, Sticker Readers, and Comic Readers—a complete literacy program with something to interest every child.

Learning to Read, Step by Step!

Ready to Read   Preschool–Kindergarten
• big type and easy words • rhyme and rhythm • picture clues
For children who know the alphabet and are eager to begin reading.

Reading with Help   Preschool–Grade 1
• basic vocabulary • short sentences • simple stories
For children who recognize familiar words and sound out new words with help.

Reading on Your Own   Grades 1–3
• engaging characters • easy-to-follow plots • popular topics
For children who are ready to read on their own.

Reading Paragraphs   Grades 2–3
• challenging vocabulary • short paragraphs • exciting stories
For newly independent readers who read simple sentences with confidence.

Ready for Chapters   Grades 2–4
• chapters • longer paragraphs • full-color art
For children who want to take the plunge into chapter books but still like colorful pictures.

STEP INTO READING® is designed to give every child a successful reading experience. The grade levels are only guides; children will progress through the steps at their own speed, developing confidence in their reading.

Remember, a lifetime love of reading starts with a single step!

Step into Reading, Random House, and the Random House colophon are registered trademarks of Penguin Random House LLC.

Visit us on the Web!
StepIntoReading.com
rhcbooks.com

Educators and librarians, for a variety of teaching tools, visit us at RHTeachersLibrarians.com

ISBN 978-0-7364-3870-4 (trade) — ISBN 978-0-7364-3871-1 (lib. bdg.)
ISBN 978-0-7364-3872-8 (ebook)

Printed in the United States of America   10 9 8 7 6

DISNEY PRINCESS

Tiana's Winter Treats

adapted by Ruth Homberg

based on the original story
by Amy Sky Koster

illustrated by the
Disney Storybook Art Team

Random House 🏠 New York

Tiana is ready
for a busy night
at her restaurant.

Tiana's Palace
is full of friends.

One day,
the weather
gets very cold.

The heater is broken.

Tiana looks
for a coat.

It is too cold
for Louis!

It is too cold
for Naveen!

No one wants

to go out.

Tiana misses

her friends.

That night,
Tiana walks outside.
It is snowing!

Tiana loves snow!

It makes the cold fun.

The snow looks
like sugar.

Tiana has an idea.

She will have

a winter party!

She bakes sweet treats.

The treats smell yummy.

Even Louis notices!

Tiana sets out

treats and warm drinks.

Louis plays music.

Tiana's friends come!

She greets her guests.

Tiana and her friends
make snow angels.

The band plays.

Everyone cheers.

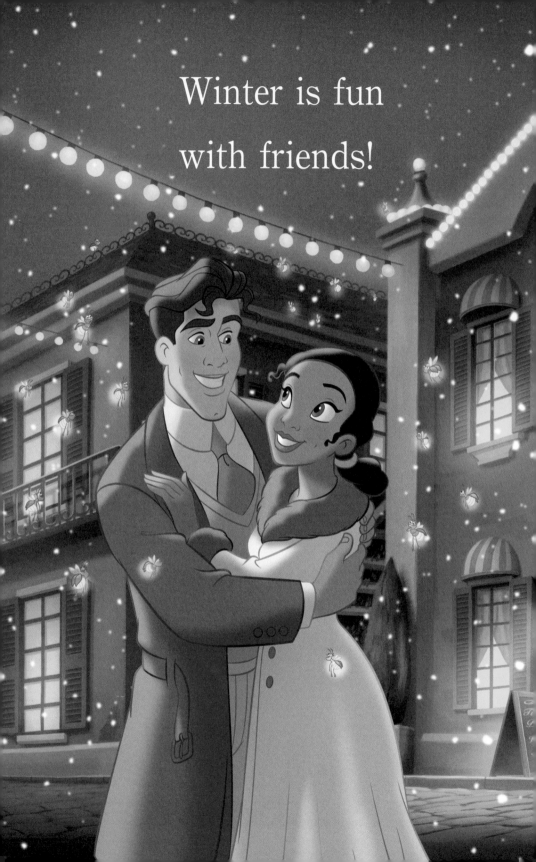

Winter is fun
with friends!